The Ghost Hunter

and the

Ghost of the Amazon Warrior

by Trish Kline and Mary Doner

Webscene art by John Droney

The Ghost Hunter and the Ghost of the Amazon Warrior
©February 2003 Ghost Hunter Productions.

Ghost Hunter Productions
P. O. Box 1199
Helena, Montana 59624
www.theghosthunteronline.com

ISBN 0-9717234-1-9
First Printing
Printed in Canada

About this book...

Books in the **Ghost Hunter** series are unlike any other books you have ever read! What makes them different is their interactive webscenes! Throughout **Ghost Hunter** books, you will be given web links. These web links are called *webscenes.*

When you go to these links, you will find images that are *very much* a part of the story. Sometimes, the images will be like illustrations in a book. Other times, the images may include puzzles to solve. Now and then, the webscene may include video or audio. You'll never know what is on the webscene... unless you go there!

If you do not visit the webscene, you will miss important facts about the story! So, be sure to visit each webscene!

Remember that, if you do not have a computer at home, you can use one at your school or city library. Or, you can ask friends to use theirs. Then, you can enjoy **Ghost Hunter** books together!

Share the adventure!

Chapter One

Cori struggled to set up the huge red umbrella.

"Great!" Cori mumbled aloud. "I finally get a day to sunbathe and the wind blows like a hurricane! Oh, no!" Cori exclaimed as her blanket took off like a tumbleweed, rolling down the Malibu beach.

Just then, her cell phone beeped. It was a message from Marta: Check your email.

Terrific, thought Cori. Now I have an excuse to give up the fight with this umbrella!

Cori opened her computer and pulled up the email from Marta:

> **Cori**
>
> **Hope you're getting to spend some time on the beach.**
>
> **Me? I've been reading some cool things on the Internet! Want to hear? (Of course you do!)**

In the 1800s, doctors didn't like to get close enough to dead people – like listening to their hearts or anything – to figure out if they were dead. Probably afraid of getting the same disease that killed the person. So, they just buried them. But the people weren't always really dead! Sometimes they were in comas. They would wake up during the funeral!

People totally freaked when the "dead" person would sit up and climb out of the coffin! People became afraid of being buried alive. So, loved ones of the deceased would drill a small hole in the lid of the coffin. They would wrap a string around the dead person's finger. Then, run the

string through the hole, tying it to
a bell outside the coffin. That way,
if the person woke up after the
coffin was sealed, they could ring
the bell and let people know they
were really alive inside!
Marta,
Virtual Sidekick of the Ghost Hunter

Cori smiled at the email from her best friend.

"Where does she find this stuff!" Cori muttered
shaking her head. But she did like getting messages
from Marta. It was just like having Marta right there
with her, instead of more than a thousand miles away.
Cori began to type a letter back.

Email
From Cori
To Marta
That's cool! I think I'll be
buried with my cell phone – just in

case. Mom's off getting us lunch
right now. She's been working on a
bunch of South American Indian
artifacts. They found lots of stuff
at a dig and shipped it here to the
university. Mom's helping them
sort out what they've got.

    And – yes – I'm on the beach!

Cori stopped typing to look up at the ocean. She expected to see just another dude breaking a wave on another neon lime green surfboard. But this wasn't just another dude! She started typing to Marta again as fast as she could.

    Hope you're still at your computer!
    Get ready to download some images.
    Call me on my cell phone as soon as
    you're ready. Make it fast!
    The Ghost Hunter

Cori clicked the send button for the email. Then, she hunted through her backpack for her Pink Diamond Girls baseball cap. She clipped the camera to the bill of the cap. Just when she finished popping the cell phone's earpiece into her ear, it rang.

"Cori, here. That you?"

"Yep," answered Marta.

"Wait until you see this!" Cori said excitedly.

"It's just now loading. Give me a sec," Marta told her friend.

"It's so cool!" Cori continued. "And, it's riding the surf right toward me!"

"Got it!" Marta shouted as the image came up on her computer screen. "Whoa!"

**To see the image that Cori and Marta saw,
go online to the webscene at:
www.TheGhostHunterOnline.com/webscene2-1**

Chapter Two

"I'm not seeing it anymore. Have you lost the image?" Cori asked Marta.

"Yep," Marta confirmed. "But I stored it on my computer so we can look at it again later if we need to."

"So, think you can find out any information on who the ghost might be?" Cori asked, already knowing what her friend would say.

"A need for knowledge? Not a problem! I'll email you when I have something," Marta replied, barely able to hide her excitement over the unfolding adventure.

"Great!" Cori told her friend. "Mom's on her way back with lunch. You know how ghost hunting makes me hungry! Catch you later," she said, ending the call.

Dr. Denton arrived with sandwiches and chips. She sat down on the sand next to her daughter.

"You and Marta been busy?" Dr. Denton asked,

nodding toward the Pink Diamond Girls cap and camera on Cori's head.

"We sure have. But I'm not sure exactly what it was we saw," Cori told her mother.

"Well, what did it look like?" her mom asked, unwrapping a sandwich.

"It's hard to describe," Cori replied. "Let me see if I can show you." Cori began to dig into the sand, making a pile out of it.

"Let's see. It was like this," Cori said as she tried to form the sand into a shape. "Sort of floating over the water."

Dr. Denton tilted her head to one side, then the other. She walked around the sand pile and stared at it as she ate her lunch.

"You saw a hamster floating in a hot air balloon over the ocean?" she asked.

"Don't you know a ghost when you see one?" Cori replied, upset at her lack of artist skills.

"Oh, a ghost floating in a hot air balloon!" Dr.

Denton said jokingly, not trying too hard to be helpful.

"It just needs a little work," Cori said as she began to reshape the sand.

"You work on it, honey. I'll go get us some drinks," she told her daughter. "Be right back."

Cori's computer beeped an incoming message.

> **Email**
> **From Marta**
> **To Cori**
>
> I did some quick web surfing. Our ghost sure looked like some sort of ancient warrior. After doing just a little research, I have already decided that history hasn't given women their due as conquering warriors! Most of the time, women fought because they wanted to help defend their homes and families. Other times, they fought

because the men were gone, either dead or off hunting food. The women had no choice but to fight. But, some tribes were led by women who created their own armies. WOMEN ONLY need apply!

Africa had thousands of female warriors. Their leaders were women, usually the queen of the tribe.

In 1624, when the king of Angola died, his sister became queen. Her name was Nzingha. Well, first thing, the ruler of Portugal broke his treaty with the country of Angola. I guess he thought that, since the king was dead and a woman was ruler, the country would be easy to invade. When the Portuguese army arrived, Queen Nzingha was ready.

Her army, made up of mostly women, fought the invaders for eleven years! Of course, during that time, the queen's army was also fighting and conquering other African kingdoms. This made her kingdom huge and much harder for the Portuguese to defeat. They finally gave up. In 1635, they ran on back to Portugal. Queen Nzingha enjoyed her victory and vast empire until the old age of 81.

Also in the 1600s, the African warrior-queen Mussasa led her warriors to so many victories, her empire covered most of the Congo! When she died, her daughter took over her mother's kingdom.

Cool, huh?

Marta

Ring! Ring!

"The Ghost Hunter," Cori laughed into the phone. "Couldn't wait for me to call you, huh?"

"Not when there are ghosts to hunt," Marta laughed back.

"The stuff about women warriors was cool," Cori said. "This ghost sure looks like someone I wouldn't want to fight!"

"These women warriors all have one thing in common. It didn't matter where they lived or who they were fighting for or against, they were usually called Amazons. There were lots of other Amazon warriors in Africa," Marta continued about the Amazon queens. "One queen named Egee led an army of women into Libya and Asia. She warred against the king of Troy in Greece. After defeating the army, she killed the king and took all the royal gold and jewels. But, on the way back home to Africa, her ships got caught in a storm. She and her ships of loot ended up on the floor of the Mediterranean Sea."

"Well, guess that could be our ghost," Cori thought out loud. "She is wearing animal skins like an African warrior might. And, she probably died in a storm at sea. That would explain her popping up over the waves. But it sure would be a long journey from the Mediterranean Sea in the Eastern Hemisphere, across the Atlantic Ocean and around to the Pacific Ocean in the Western Hemisphere."

"Guess she needed the best ghost hunter she could find," laughed Marta. "No distance too far to go for the best!"

"Thanks," Cori said, trying to be modest. "But, ghosts don't usually leave home – whether it's the house where they lived, battlefields where they fought or the ship that sank their bodies to the bottom of the ocean. When Mom came back with lunch, I tried to show her what the ghost looked like…"

"What did you show her?" Marta asked.

"I made a sand sculpture. See?" Cori said proudly, dipping her head to point the camera toward the sand sculpture. "What do you think?"

Marta laughed as the image streamed onto her computer screen.

"That bad?" Cori asked, staring at the pile of sand.

"Let's just say… you have a gift. It's seeing ghosts. Leave the artistic stuff for someone else," Marta told her friend.

"Ok. I'm giving up sand sculpting. Email me the image of the ghost so Mom can look at it," Cori gave in.

"I'm sending it right now," Marta said. "That may help your mom figure out who our ghost is."

Cori looked out over the waves lapping on the beach.

"I'm sure she can," Cori said. "But, for right now, I think I better DUCK!"

**To see what made Cori duck,
go online to the webscene at:
www.TheGhostHunterOnline.com/webscene2-2**

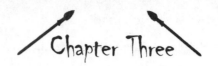
"Cori! Cori! You ok?" Marta shouted. "All I can see is sand."

Cori wiggled her fingers in front of the camera lens.

"I had to take a dive into some kid's sand castle. A dart went whizzing past me," she told her friend. "I'm still spitting sand, but I'm ok."

"Is she gone?" Marta wanted to know.

"Yeah," Cori told her. "Gone for now. Did you see it all on your end?"

"Most of it. Up until you decided to go play in the sand," Marta teased her. "I'll send you the images right now."

"Good. Cause I want to have Mom take a look at them," Cori replied.

———

"Hmm," Dr. Denton studied the pictures. "Looks

like a blowgun."

"A glow gun? What's a glow gun?" Marta spoke into Cori's earpiece.

"Not glow gun," Cori answered. "Blowgun. You know, long hollow stick that you use to blow poison darts at people."

"Oh," Marta laughed at the misunderstanding. "You've got to get a better mic. This one makes it so hard to eavesdrop."

"Sometimes the darts are dipped in poison," Dr. Denton picked up on her daughter's comment. "Poison darts were used mostly for hunting animals or birds. But, sometimes, the poison darts were used to kill human enemies," Dr. Denton added. "Matter of fact, several tribes in South America still use poison darts even today."

"So, does that mean our ghost is from South America?" Cori asked.

"Not necessarily," Dr. Denton began. "Long ago, tribes across much of the world used blowguns. Even a

15

few tribes in North America used blowguns. The Japanese used blowguns centuries ago. Ninjas were some of the first warriors to use blowguns in warfare. Then, of course, there were the terrible Dayks pirates. They were known for their poison barbed darts."

"Poison barbed darts!" exclaimed Cori.

"Yes, the end had a barb, like on barbed wire fence. If you tried to pull the dart out, the barb broke off, leaving the poisoned tip inside the wound."

"Where did they get the poison?" Cori asked, her interest growing at the mention of Ninjas and pirates.

"Some plants are poisonous," Dr. Denton went on. "They could boil such a plant and dip their darts into the mixture. But the best poison to use was frogs."

"Frogs!" exclaimed Cori.

"Yeah," chimed in Marta. "I remember reading about that when our class studied the South American rain forest. There are over 170 different kinds of poisonous frogs. Cute little guys! Red, green, yellow, some have spots, others have stripes. The best for poison are the Blue frogs. They are really packed for poison! The poison covers his entire body to protect it. We sweat water from the pores in our skin. The Blue frog sweats poison. Anyway, warriors needed to rub the tips of their darts over the sticky skin on the frog's back. But the frog wasn't very big on sitting still for this dart-rubbing ceremony. So, the warriors would have to kill the little guys first."

"Uh-huh," Cori nodded as her friend went on and on. "Marta knows ALL about the poison dart frogs of the South American rain forest," Cori whispered to her mom to let her know what Marta was saying on the phone.

"I'm not at all surprised," her mom smiled, waiting patiently for Marta to finish sharing from her wealth of knowledge.

"Wow, thanks!" joked Cori as Marta grew silent. "And I thought getting warts from frogs was all I had to worry about!"

"Well," her mother began. "If this warrior woman is

spitting poison darts at you, I'd say warts aren't your biggest worry."

"You mean… a ghost can kill me with a poison dart!" Cori exclaimed.

"Well, I don't recall having heard of a death by poison dart delivered by ghost. But, I certainly can't rule it out. I would suggest that, if this ghost is that angry, you better be very careful not to make her any angrier," Dr. Denton warned.

"We'll keep that in mind," Cori joked weakly, remembering the sound of the dart passing by her head.

"Think we should give up on this one?" Marta asked, worried about the danger her friend might face.

"I'm not quitting," Cori replied into the cell phone.

"Well, then," Dr. Denton smiled as her daughter refused to give up. "Guess you better find out more about this warrior and why she's in such a bad mood!"

"Can you tell when she lived by the clothes she's wearing?" Cori asked her mom.

"Not for sure," Dr. Denton rubbed her chin

thoughtfully. "But, if she was a North American Indian or a South American Amazon warrior, she could have lived anywhere from a few hundred years ago to a few thousand. Sorry I can't help more than that."

"Thanks, Mom," Cori told her. "You've at least given us somewhere to start."

"Yeah, somewhere in either North or South America! A few hundred years ago… or, maybe, a few thousand years ago," Marta laughed in her friend's earpiece. "That sure narrows it down!"

"You're welcome, sweetie," Dr. Denton replied. "You, too, Marta," the woman whispered into the mic clipped to her daughter's shirt. "You two be careful now. I've got to get back to work. You might want to check out the South American stuff at the museum. Maybe it'll give you more ideas."

"A poison blowgun," Cori muttered under her breath as her mother walked away. "Not the friendliest of greetings."

"You wouldn't want to hiccup when one of those

things was loaded," Marta laughed. "Although it would definitely put an end to your hiccups! Forever!"

"Very funny," Cori replied to her friend's joke. "I'm on my way to the museum to search for clues. Coming along?"

"I'm going to get back online and see what else I can find out about women warriors," Marta said. "Call me if anything exciting happens."

"Will do," Cori answered, ending the call.

Cori walked into the storage basement of the museum. It smelled like damp earth – musky with a hint of decay. The room was full of tables filled with pottery, statues and weapons belonging to villagers who lived 500 years ago in the jungles of Brazil, South America.

Cori was familiar with the odors of recently unearthed artifacts. She had been on lots of archaeological digs with her mother. The smells from the dig sites all seemed to have one thing in common.

"Um, dead people and all that rots," Cori mumbled softly.

Her mom had said the researchers had found some human bones – even skeletons and a mummy or two. But, Cori knew those would be locked in special rooms to try to prevent the decaying process. Maybe her mom could get her into those rooms later. For now, she would have to settle for looking at cooking pots and dinner plates.

"Marta's not going to want to miss all of this," Cori said as she dialed her friend.

"Virtual Sidekick, here," Marta answered the phone. "Been looking but I haven't found much of anything yet."

"That's ok. I was just calling because I thought you might want to see what I'm looking at here," Cori explained.

"Great! Might give me some ideas of ways to go with the research," Marta added. "Put on both your front facing and rear facing cameras. That way, I can get the pictures twice as fast. I'll be ready in a sec."

"Any idea of who the ghost is would be more than we have now," Cori continued as she clipped the cameras on her cap. "Ghosts don't just show up for no reason. She's stuck between worlds and can't pass over."

"Ok. Getting pictures now. Good point. If she's from a North American Indian tribe, that would kinda explain why she's hanging around California. But, if she's a South American Amazon, she's almost 5,000 miles from her village. Why isn't she floating through the rain forest?"

"Well, maybe these artifacts will give us more clues about why she's here. Maybe it has something to do with what's been dug up and brought here. Maybe she came along with the stuff from the digs," Cori suggested.

"Ghosts do that?" asked Marta. "Hang onto stuff and go where the stuff goes?"

"Don't see why they couldn't," Cori offered.

Cori walked slowly, turning her head to scan the room.

"There," she said. "That's the big picture on all the stuff in the room. I'll start walking along the tables now and you can see each artifact."

Cori started at a nearby table and began to move alongside it, studying each artifact as she came to it.

"This crossbow sure looks wicked, doesn't it?" Cori remarked as she looked at the weapon, lowering her head and the camera for a closer look.

"What was that?" exclaimed Marta.

"A crossbow. I just told you. No need to get so excited," Cori answered calmly.

"Not the crossbow! What just flew by behind your back?" Marta continued.

"Must have been shadows," replied Cori. "No one is in here but me."

"Dead wrong, Cori!" Marta suddenly shouted into her ear. "They are standing right behind you! You are SO outnumbered!"

To see what Marta saw behind Cori,
go online to the webscene at:
www.TheGhostHunterOnline.com/webscene2-3

Chapter Four

The images on Marta's screen bounced up and down.

"The images are kinda blurry," reported Marta to her friend. "Are you still running?"

"Uh, yeah!" Cori replied, her voice gasping for air. "Wearing a ton of armor doesn't seem to slow down a ghost at all! Hold on!"

Suddenly, the image on Marta's screen brought her face-to-face with a steel wall. Then, the image bounced one last time.

"You just dove into the elevator, didn't you?" asked Marta knowingly.

"Yep," laughed Cori. "Found out with the ghost at Gettysburg that ghosts don't like to ride elevators."

"Wonder why? It would be a fast way to travel. And it beats floating upstairs. Unless they float for exercise.

But, if you're dead, do you really need all that much exercise? Seems a bit pointless to try to stay healthy if you are already dead," Marta rambled on jokingly.

"I'm so glad to know you can make jokes – even as my life hangs in the balance!" Cori gasped, trying to catch her breath.

"What life hanging in the balance?" Marta replied. "You're riding an elevator. Elevators are not all that dangerous. I have ridden many myself."

Cori leaned against the wall of the elevator. After her dash from death, the cool steel felt good against her back. She knew Marta's joking was just her friend's way of dealing with the sudden danger presented by the ghosts.

"Could be something to do with ghosts being energy," Cori reasoned.

"What could be something about ghosts being energy?" Marta questioned, happy the silence was broken.

"Elevators. Why ghosts don't like elevators. You

know how it feels when you go up fast in an elevator? You feel lighter. Then, when you go down, you feel heavier? It has to do with energy and mass and all that kind of stuff. Maybe that bothers ghosts."

"Guess that means ghosts don't ride many roller coasters, huh?" Marta laughed. "Well, these ghosts were definitely bothered. But I don't think it was about elevators. Luckily, the camera got a good shot of them before you took off on your 50-yard dash," Marta told her. "Bad news is they want to kill you. Good news is that we know who these ghosts are."

"Really? Were they wearing name tags?" Cori joked.

"Nearly as good," Marta replied. "They were wearing armor unlike any other."

"Metal helmets that turn up around the edges. Major chest armor. Weird looking pants," Cori described the ghosts who had chased her across the basement.

"Yep," said Marta. "They were Spanish conquistadors."

"So, that gives us a time period," Cori replied.

"Absolutely," answered Marta. "Spanish exploration of the Americas. It began with Christopher Columbus in 1492. Then, other explorers followed during the 1500s. Some like Cortes invaded Mexico and attacked the Aztecs."

"And others invaded and attacked people in South America," added Cori.

"You were standing in a room full of artifacts from Brazil," Marta observed.

"Artifacts from that same time period," Cori agreed.

"And don't forget two very unfriendly ghosts. But, then, I wouldn't think soldiers who went around invading countries would be known for their friendliness," Marta pointed out.

"We have a real problem here," Cori told her sidekick.

"What? Two very bad ghosts who want to see you dead?" Marta replied.

"No, not that," Cori answered matter-of-factly. "They ain't no big deal. No, I'm talking about the fact that we have two ghost appearances at almost the same time. Which do we help? The Amazon or the conquistadors?"

"Well, there are two of them and only one of her," Marta pointed out. "We'd be helping more with them."

"Yeah, but we're going for quality here, not quantity," Cori joked.

"Then I vote for whichever isn't trying to kill you," Marta suggested.

"Well, that would seem to rule out BOTH of them," Cori answered. "Unless, nail you with a blowgun dart is a special welcoming custom among Amazons."

"Since blowgun darts are dipped in poison and she was aiming a blowgun AT you," began Marta. "I think we can rule out that her greeting was 'so glad you showed up on my beach!' "

"Maybe we just misunderstood her actions," suggested Cori.

"Ghosts just hate being misunderstood," Marta laughed. "Yeah, you're right. Probably was a friendly poison dart. After all, dart poisons don't always kill. I read that some poisons are ingredients that doctors use to put you to sleep during heart operations."

"Somehow she doesn't look like a heart doctor, either," Cori joked back. "So, what… are you reading medical journals now?"

"My older sister Rosa is in med school," Marta answered. "She emails me about all the cool stuff. Can't wait until she gets her cadaver!"

"Cadaver?" Cori repeated.

"Yeah, the dead bodies they use in med school so the students can learn the body parts," Marta explained.

"Back to the ghosts?" Cori asked.

"Good idea!" Marta agreed. "Go back and give the ol' girl another shot at it!"

"Go back? It? It – as in me?" asked Cori. "You want me to give her another chance to spit a dart between my eyes?"

"It – as in helping us understand her," answered Marta. "Give her another shot at trying to tell us what her problem is. Help us know how to help her. Give us some ideas why she's here. But, this time, wear the second camera. Maybe it will help me pick up more details about what is going on around you when she appears."

"Oh, yeah, right. Go back and see if the Amazon warrior feels like chit-chatting about her troubling life on the other side. Of course. Why didn't I think of that?" laughed Cori as she ended the call. "Ring you back when I reach the beach."

———————

It was dark by the time Cori got back to the beach. A full moon shone on the water. The wind that had blown all day was now silent. Cori sat down in the cool sand and connected the cameras to her Diamond Girls cap. Then, she called Marta.

"Hooked up and good for ghost," Cori told Marta as she answered.

"Great. So how do you make a ghost show?" Marta asked.

"I don't make ghosts show," laughed Cori. "Remember that science experiment with the magnet, how the paper clips were drawn to it? Well, that's kinda how it is with me and ghosts. I show up at a haunting and they are just drawn to me."

"They're just attracted to you, huh?" Marta teased.

"I just pull them in," Cori joked back.

"Guess that makes you a ghost magnet," Marta laughed at the comparison.

"Must be – because here she comes again!" Cori explained, tilting her head toward the ocean. "Can you see her?"

"Shucks! All dressed up for battle and nobody to kill," responded Marta. "Unless, of course, that's why she's so drawn to you."

"Finding out what's troubling the ol' girl," laughed Cori. "Does that come before or after the running for my life part?"

"Well, she doesn't seem in a huge hurry to blow you away," Marta offered, noticing that the Amazon's blowgun was not yet aimed at her friend's head. "Go on. See if she wants to chat."

Cori walked slowly down the beach toward the Amazon. The Amazon warrior continued to float above the water.

"She doesn't seem to be afraid of me," Cori whispered to Marta.

"Afraid of you?" Marta gave a weak laugh. "You're wearing a pink baseball cap and a backpack. She's an Amazon warrior… blowgun, bow and arrow, war mask, spear. Which part of pink cap and backpack is supposed to be making her shake in her moccasins?"

"Ok, well, afraid might not be the exact phrase to describe what's going through her mind," Cori admitted.

"Total confusion pops to my mind," Marta replied.

"There has to be some way that we can figure out what's going on with her. Why is she here?" Cori talked as she walked closer and closer to the Amazon warrior. "Why is she appearing to me? How can we even tell if she's a good spirit or bad…?"

"Good ghost, bad ghost will have to wait," interrupted Marta. "I've got some images coming in on the second camera. That running for your life part? Now may be a good time to just go with that feeling!"

"What is it?" Cori asked as she turned to see what Marta had seen behind her. "Ok, this isn't good, but no need to panic."

"No? Then, maybe you want to take a look back at the Amazon," Marta said as images streamed into her computer from the other camera. "Let me know when the need to panic arrives."

Cori looked from one end of the beach to the other. Then, back again. The cameras were streaming images fast and furious across Marta's computer screen.

"News flash," Cori whispered to her virtual sidekick. "Need to panic has arrived."

**To see Cori's major danger on the beach,
go to the webscene at:
www.TheGhostHunterOnline.com/webscene2-4**

33

Chapter Five

"Did you see that?" Marta shouted. "That was so cool!"

"Extremely cool!" agreed Cori. "Those guys are really afraid of her!"

"Would on her bad side be somewhere you'd like to be?" Marta kidded her friend. "Guess this solves our problem about who we should help," Marta said.

"It sure does," Cori agreed. "The Amazon!"

"Yeah, when someone steps up, ready to save your life, no doubt whose side we're going to take! Allegiance to the Amazon!" Marta agreed. "So what do we do now?"

"Guess we should try to figure out why two big, brave, covered-in-armor-from-head-to-foot conquistadors run in terror from a woman in animal skins carrying a blowgun. Sure she's an Amazon warrior but still…" Cori wondered.

"Yeah, the way they took off… I'm willing to bet this wasn't their first meeting. They sure didn't want to have anything to do with her again! We've got to find out about conquistadors and what happened when they invaded South America," Marta said. "I'll send you an email as soon as I find anything. What are you going to do?"

"Go home and shower!" Cori laughed. "I feel like half the beach is stuck to my skin! Check ya later."

"Ditto," Marta concluded, hanging up the receiver.

Cori. You Have Mail!

> **Email**
> **From Marta**
> **To Cori**
> **The biggest thing driving Spanish conquistadors was greed. Since before Columbus, people in Europe wanted to find a shorter route to India and the rest of the**

Far East to get spices. Food's
pretty boring without them.

But explorers like Columbus
didn't find a new way to India when
they sailed west across the Atlantic
Ocean. North and South America
were in the way! So they started
looking for spices there instead.
One thing the conquistadors were
looking for in South America was
cinnamon, la canela they call it.
Pretty dumb, since cinnamon only
grew in the Far East!

"Yeah, well I don't think these guys were known for
their high IQs!" Cori laughed to herself.

But the conquistadors didn't
just want spices. Most of all, they
wanted gold. LOTS of gold. Once

they found gold, they were supposed to ship it back to the King of Spain. But they also got a share of whatever they found. The more gold they found, the richer they would be.

They were all over South America trying to find a city of gold they had heard stories about. They heard the city was ruled by a king named El Dorado. (That's Spanish for one major golden guy!) People said he was so rich he covered himself in gold dust every day and washed it off every night. Didn't even bother with clothes! Whenever conquistadors came to a new place, they would question the Indians about El Dorado. To get the conquistadors to leave them

**alone, the people would say the
city of gold was a couple days
journey away from them. Note to
self: conquistadors not the
sharpest knives in the drawer! The
Indians fooled those dumb, greedy
guys every time because the
soldiers always moved on! They
were CRAZY with wanting to find
that city and the king.**

"How dumb can you get? Believing in a whole city
made of gold, ruled by a naked guy who uses gold dust
like baby powder?" thought Cori.

**Some conquistadors in South
America were led by this guy
named Francisco de Orellana.
They were stuck in the jungle
starving to death – surrounded by**

food like birds and monkeys. That's because these guys had no idea how to hunt. They were too noisy clunking around in their armor. They hacked through the underbrush instead of sneaking up quiet. They got so hungry they even boiled their shoes and pieces of their saddles to make soup!

"I was wrong," Cori laughed to herself. "Dumber and dumber!"

So, Orellana built a couple boats to go look for food. He spent eight months floating down a river all the way to the Atlantic Ocean! (They tried to go back the way they came but the river's current was too strong and fast to go against it.)

Along their voyage down the
river, they raided Indian villages.
They found a little gold, but no
city of gold. They killed lots of
Indians, stole their food and
anything else they wanted to take.
These guys were nasty!

"Too dumb to sneak up and shoot a rabbit for
dinner," Cori mumbled to herself. "So, instead, they just
killed a whole village of people to take their food. Men
their mothers could be proud of, no doubt!"

Orellana said he found women
warriors on his river journey. He
called them Amazons. He wanted
to name the big river after himself.
Back in Spain, the royal guys in
charge liked the Amazon warrior

story so much they changed the name to the Amazon River. It's one of the biggest rivers in the world. It flows across almost all of South America, nearly 4,000 miles! The mouth of the river where it empties into the Atlantic Ocean is more than 200 miles wide! And check this out – the Amazon River is the home of the world's fiercest fish. They're called piranhas and they have very sharp teeth. They travel together in groups of about 20 fish. They form a circle around another fish and attack! Eating them in just a few seconds! If a bird gets too close to the water, feathers go flying! They even eat cattle that wander into the river. They just bite off pieces from the legs and

the cow falls down into the water.
A few minutes and the cow is
history. Kinda gives a whole new
meaning to fast food!

Marta

Ring! Ring!

"Loved the research!" Cori began. "Fast food?"

"Just trying to bring a little humor into my writing," Marta joked back. "A little personal touch."

"Ok, so what do we have?" Cori asked her virtual sidekick. "We've got conquistadors. We've got a woman warrior."

"I think we're on the right track," Marta concluded. "Let's head back to the museum and check out the stuff there again."

"I think that's our best bet, too," Cori agreed. "I'll call you up when I'm ready to send some images."

———————

Cori opened the door of the basement storage room.

"Check it out first," Marta warned in her ear. "Let's make sure the conquistadors aren't planning a surprise party for you."

"Right," Cori agreed, slowly peering around the corner. "Coast is clear."

"Let's try some of the stuff we haven't looked at yet," Marta suggested.

Cori moved quickly past the tables filled with pottery.

"This table seems to have weapons and stuff like that. This looks like an arrowhead," Cori said, picking up a flat, pointed stone.

"What's that next to it?" Marta wanted to know.

"This?" Cori said, picking up the object. "It looks like a small scrap of animal skin of some sort."

Cori turned the artifact over in her hand. She leaned her head nearer to it so Marta could get a better image from the camera.

"Oooh, rotten old animal skin – up close and personal!" Marta laughed as the image grew on her monitor.

Cori again began to move along the table, but she didn't get far.

"We have company," she announced to Marta, turning her head and camera to capture the image of the visitor.

The Amazon stood a few feet from Cori surrounded by a white mist.

"Yeah," Marta whispered. "I see her. No blowgun. So far, so good. But maybe you'd better put down the animal skin – just in case."

Cori put the skin back on the table and slowly stepped away from it. The warrior floated slowly toward Cori, her arm outstretched.

"Maybe I should have put it down a lot quicker," Cori said, taking another step backward.

When the ghost reached the table, she stretched her hand over the skin. The mist around her began to swirl and change colors.

"Cori!" Marta whispered. "What's happening?"

"Pretty cool, huh?" Cori whispered back to her sidekick.

"Yeah! It looks like you're in the middle of a jungle!" Marta said excitedly.

The entire room had suddenly changed. A vision appeared in the mist round about the Amazon. Large, jungle trees were everywhere. The sounds of a large river flowing nearby broke the silence. Huts slowly began to appear – one by one – until an entire village filled the room.

"I think we're entering the Amazon's reality," Cori explained. "Something about that animal skin has taken her to a day in her life."

"And we get to go along for the ride," concluded Marta. "I've never entered a vision before."

"Entering visions – the ghost's reality – is pretty common," Cori answered matter-of-factly. "This may be your first but it won't be your last. Think we are in South America?" Cori asked in a whisper.

"Yeah, probably around the 1500s. That's the date

your mom said the researchers put on the artifacts from this dig," Marta replied. "Where are you going?"

"Over there behind those big ferns. That's where the Amazon seems to be hiding and watching," Cori answered. "Figure, if she wants to hide, I better want to hide, too!"

Cori knelt down near where the Amazon ghost was huddled behind a fern. Suddenly, something began to pull Cori toward the inside of the vision.

"Whoa!" Cori yelled as she grabbed onto a nearby table leg.

"What's happening?" exclaimed Marta, sensing the danger.

"It's the vision!" Cori replied, wrapping both arms around the leg of the heavy steel display table full of artifacts. "The vision is sucking the Amazon into it! It feels like a tornado is swirling by, trying to suck me into it!"

Marta watched her monitor. The scene did look like a tornado. She could see the images in the vision swirling about like they were being sucked into a bottle. The Amazon ghost was suddenly yanked from her hiding place behind the fern. In a split second, the ghost was whipped through the air, across the room and into the vision.

Then, the room went calm.

"Could you see what happened?" Cori asked, letting go of her death-hold on the table leg.

"Every detail via the camera on the back of your cap!" answered Marta excitedly. "The Amazon was sucked into the vision. And, then the vision got sort of blurry… but look! The vision! It's getting clear again! What was all that about anyway?"

"My guess is that the Amazon wasn't an observer of that event but a participant," Cori explained. "In other words, the event that she was looking at in the vision, she had actually been in that event."

"Ok, so, her spirit couldn't be in two places at the same time," Marta reasoned aloud.

"Exactly," Cori agreed. "The vision appeared. The

events were unfolding. And something was about to happen in the vision exactly as it had in her life. She was there – a part of whatever happened."

"So, since her spirit was there in the vision, it couldn't be here in the room with you watching it happen," Marta concluded. "Her spirit couldn't be in two places at the same time. Guess that means we'll be seeing her in the vision."

Cori knelt back down behind the ferns and waited. The bend of the river came into sight. Around the bend came a large boat, filled with conquistadors.

"Here we go!" whispered Marta with excitement as the image of the boat full of conquistadors came into focus on her screen.

The boat neared the shore. The soldiers jumped off, guns and swords in hand. Shouting, they ran toward the village. At the sound of the invaders' shouts, the Indians came out of their huts.

One of the conquistadors grabbed an Indian. "Dondé está El Dorado!" he shouted at the man.

"What's he saying?" Cori whispered to Marta.

"It's Spanish. It means where is El Dorado!" whispered Marta.

The Indian did not answer. The conquistador hit the Indian and knocked him down. Other conquistadors grabbed more of the villagers and questioned them. The Indians did not answer the soldiers. With each Indian's silence, the soldiers became more and more angry. Finally, out of patience at not getting the answers they wanted, they beat the Indians.

"Cori, is that a fire?" Marta asked, fearing for her friend's life. "Is the basement on fire?"

"No, it's not the basement," Cori replied. "The flames are coming from the vision. The soldiers have set fire to the huts. They are burning the village to the ground."

"What about the Indians?" Marta asked, trying to peer through the smoky images on her screen. "Can you see the Indians? Are they all right?"

"I don't see anyone," Cori whispered. "Wait. There's

the Amazon."

"What is she staring at?" Marta asked. "Can you get closer for a better look?"

"Yeah," Cori answered softly. "But you really don't want to see this."

Marta watched as the horror of the scene appeared on her screen.

To see what Cori knew Marta wouldn't
want to see, go to the webscene at:
www.TheGhostHunterOnline.com/webscene2-5

Chapter Six

"How could they have done that!" Marta exclaimed.

"Because they wanted gold," Cori shook her head. "Like your research said, conquistadors destroyed village after village, taking whatever they wanted…"

"And killing everyone who didn't give them what they wanted – a roadmap to the city of gold!" Marta said angrily.

"They would have probably killed them even if the Indians told them where the gold was and dug it up for them," Cori suggested. "Remember the Aztecs? They gave up all of their gold and the conquistadors killed them anyway. I just don't see why they had to decapitate them like that."

"Because decapitation was a very common message soldiers left for whoever might happen by villages that they had conquered," Marta explained. "The message was… mess with us and we will kill you… then cut off your head and leave it for the buzzards! No wonder the Amazon is stuck and can't cross over! She must be reliving that scene over and over," Marta concluded.

"As awful as it was, I don't think it's enough to keep her here," Cori reasoned. "She was a warrior. She would have seen things like that many times."

"True," Marta agreed. "But maybe she's feeling guilty because she didn't do anything to stop them."

"Maybe. But how could she? She was one person. There were a couple dozen of them," Cori reasoned.

"Then something else must be holding her here," Marta said.

"Yeah," agreed Cori. "Now we just have to figure out what it is."

"Well figure fast!" encouraged Marta. "Cause the vision is going… and… ok, there! The Amazon is gone, too!"

The vision of the jungle disappeared as quickly as it had appeared. Cori was again standing in the dimly lit, dusty basement.

"If handling that piece of animal skin brought her out once, maybe we can bring her back," Cori reasoned, picking up the animal skin.

Cori waited but no one appeared.

"Maybe you have to rub it," Marta suggested.

"It's not a genie in a bottle," laughed Cori. "Besides, I didn't rub it the first time."

"Ok, so maybe it's one vision per item," Marta continued. "Pick up something else."

Cori slowly began to pick up artifacts from the tables. One by one she handled all the artifacts in the room.

"That's the last one," she sighed to Marta after an hour. "Nothing is bringing her back."

"So, we give up?" asked Marta.

"We've run out of artifacts," Cori pointed out. "We're at a dead end."

"Not completely," answered Marta.

"What do you mean?" Cori asked. "I've tried every

one. Held it. Turned it over. Even rubbed most of them! No ghost. No vision."

"There's another dead end we can follow… Didn't you say that there is another room – a room filled with dead people's bones? " Marta said.

"That's right! I'll have to give Mom a call and ask her to get me in. The university is pretty picky about who they let in there. But I'm sure Mom can help," Cori said. "I'll give you a call back after I talk with her."

———————

"Your mom is so cool! Helping you get in to look at all this stuff," Marta said, watching the images of skulls and skeletons stream onto her computer monitor.

"Yeah, Mom is pretty cool," Cori said proudly, moving her head and the camera on her cap from table to table. "But she feels I have a calling to be a ghost hunter. She wants me to do what it is I'm supposed to do," Cori added as she picked up a leg bone.

"And the coolest part is she helps but she doesn't interfere," Marta agreed. "She lets you do it all yourself."

"Well, me and my virtual sidekick!" joked Cori.

"We make a good team – I handle the computer; you handle the bones," Marta laughed back.

"How about this one?" Cori picked up part of a rib and held it, looking around the room.

"Stir up a vision?" Marta asked.

"Nope. Nothing," Cori said after a moment.

For 15 minutes, Cori picked up bone after bone. When at last she picked up a skull, the room began to change.

"That's using your head!" Marta teased.

"Here she is!" Cori said excitedly as the Amazon faded into view a few feet away.

Cori placed the head back on the table and stepped away. The warrior moved closer, her arm extended.

The skull rose from the table and floated in the air. The Amazon grabbed the skull and pulled it near to her.

"She looks really sad," Marta said.

Cori and Marta watched as the room moved and

changed colors and shape.

"Back to the jungle," Cori whispered.

"Where's the Amazon?" Marta asked.

"She's walking into the jungle. See?" Cori turned her head just in time for the camera to catch sight of the Amazon disappearing into the forest. "She's part of the vision now."

"Wow. No tornado this time," Marta noted. "She just walked into the vision. Must be somewhere she wants to get back to."

"Or the place she can't get away from," added Cori.

"I don't think this is the same village as the other vision," Marta whispered. "It's bigger. Has more huts."

Within moments, once again Cori and Marta watched as two conquistador boats floated down the river toward the village. This time, however, no one came out of the huts.

The conquistadors jumped on shore from the boats. Some of them went into the huts, but they came out alone.

"Where are all the villagers?" Marta asked softly.

"I think the conquistadors are about to find out," Cori said. "Look!"

Suddenly the jungle came alive! A shower of arrows flew out of the thick growth of plants near the river. Several of the conquistadors fell down as they were hit.

Women warriors poured out from behind the thick jungle trees where they had hidden. Leading the warriors was the Amazon ghost.

"She must be the queen of the warriors!" Cori said.

"Wow!" Marta exclaimed. "Our ghost is Queen of the Amazons!"

The queen wore a large feathered headdress and carried a spear in one hand. With her other hand she raised her blowgun to her lips. She fired a poison dart. It ZIPPED and struck a conquistador in the neck.

The conquistadors were taken by surprise. Warriors ran and grabbed the soldiers. Some ran spears into the invaders' armor. Others used knives and fought the men in hand-to-hand combat.

"That metal armor is thick and heavy. The women

can't pierce it with their knives!" Marta said.

"You're right. But the women can move a lot faster than the men. All that armor slows them down," Cori observed, watching the fighting continue.

The conquistadors could not move as fast or easily as the women could. The men tried to use their swords to slash and stab the women. But the women warriors were quick and able to jump out of the way.

The few conquistadors left on the boat began to fire guns.

"Guns!" Marta said. "The Amazons can't out run a gun! They've probably never even seen a gun before."

The Amazon queen looked stunned to see fire explode from the sticks the men held. She watched as one of her warriors fell to the ground, dead from the gun blast.

With a loud scream, the queen ran to the boat and jumped on board. She attacked the man who had fired the gun that killed the warrior.

Other conquistadors tried to hold her back, but she

fought them, too. One slashed her arm with his sword, but that only made the queen angrier.

Two conquistadors struggled with the Amazon queen at the edge of the boat. Quickly, other Amazon warriors followed the lead of their queen. They swarmed on board the boat, fighting more conquistadors.

As one of the women warriors cried out, the other warriors turned toward where the queen was battling the two conquistadors.

"Look out!" Cori shouted, knowing even as the words left her mouth that they would do no good to change events in a battle fought more than 500 years ago.

"Her warriors can't help her," Marta said sadly. "And neither can we."

To see what happened to the Amazon warrior queen, go to the webscene at: www.TheGhostHunterOnline.com/webscene2-6

Chapter Seven

"She never had a chance," Marta said quietly.

The vision disappeared. All the women warriors and conquistadors faded away. The river and the village were gone. The room was once again just a room filled with bones.

"Yeah," Cori agreed. "This has got to be what's holding her here. But why?"

"I'll see if I can find anything else out about the fight," Marta suggested.

"I'm going to look around here. There may be clues that will help us out. Later," Cori said as she hung up.

"Maybe it's time to try a different room," Cori mumbled to herself. "I know Mom said they had LOTS of stuff they haven't sorted yet."

Cori walked down the hall.

"Closet," she laughed as she opened the first door.

"I doubt the conquistadors used floor mops as weapons."

She continued to try doors.

"This is more like it," Cori smiled as she opened another door. "Looks like pieces of armor and weapons."

Cori walked next to the tables, studying what was there. On one table was a soldier's helmet. The museum people hadn't cleaned it yet. It was still rusty and had a dent on one side. Next to it was a knife with half of the blade gone.

Broken weapons can't hurt anyone anymore, thought Cori to herself. But, as she glanced around the room, Cori saw a long spear began to rise from the table and float in the air!

"Ok. Maybe this room wasn't such a good idea," Cori said, backing toward the door.

Other weapons also began to move. A sword. A crossbow. Followed by the images of the two conquistador ghosts fading into view. The ghosts held the weapons – pointed in Cori's direction!

The conquistador with the crossbow raised it to his shoulder and took aim.

Cori yanked open the door and slammed it behind her.

ZIP! SPRONG!

She heard the arrow stick in the door behind her.

"Elevator time!" Cori said as she took off at a run down the hall.

The elevator doors were closed when she reached them. Looking over her shoulder, she saw the two conquistadors coming down the hall after her. She pushed the call button on the elevator over and over.

"Come ON!" she yelled, willing the doors open.

She turned to see the conquistador again raise his crossbow and point it at her.

The door slid silently open and Cori dove inside.

WHOOSH! THUD! came the arrow!

DING! went the elevator as it rose up with Cori safely inside.

Beep! Beep!

Cori pulled out her phone to find a message on the

screen from Marta: Check your email.

"Sorry, guys," she spoke to the closed door. "Like to play more but I've gotta check my email. You guys wouldn't know anything about that since you've been dead for about 500 years!"

Cori stepped off the elevator in the lobby of the museum. She quickly removed her computer from her backpack. Her message from Marta was waiting.

> **Cori**
>
> **Took a lot of digging, but here's what I've got. One of the conquistadors wrote about it in his journal.**
>
> **On June 24, 1542 there was a BIG fight between Orellana's conquistadors and the Amazons. These warriors were GREAT with bows and arrows with copper tips. The Amazons fired so many arrows**

into Orellana's boat he said it looked like a porcupine!

Orellana said there were about a dozen Amazons who led the other Indians. He also said the Spanish killed seven or eight of the Amazons.

That must have made the Indians pretty mad. They chased the conquistadors down the river! Orellana didn't get a chance to ask them about El Dorado or steal any of their food or kill any more of them. He must have been REALLY MAD when a bunch of women beat all his big, bad conquistadors like that!

Word spread down the river how the Amazons beat Orellana. After that, he avoided land

because Indians from other villages
waited along the river to attack the
soldiers whenever they came near!

Sounds like our Amazon queen
showed the villages how to beat
back the conquistadors. She
helped put Orellana on the run.

Virtual Sidekick

Ring! Ring!

"It's me," Cori identified herself as Marta said hello.
"All I found out was that the conquistadors are still as
bad on that side as they were on this."

"Out visiting the dead without me?" Marta joked.

"I was checking out some artifacts – until our two
Spanish ghosts showed up. Those guys just pop up out
of nowhere!" Cori chuckled.

"What were you doing to make them show?" asked
Marta, unhappy she had missed seeing the conquistadors.

"Nothing! Really!" Cori replied. "I was in a room

with armor and old broken weapons. But, I didn't even touch anything! Suddenly, spears and swords are floating into the air. The bad guys pop in! One has a crossbow. I run for the elevator. Then I hear the arrow hit the door."

"Ok, you are going to have to stop going to these surprise parties alone," Marta sounded like a mother. "You need someone to watch your back. And, from the sounds of it, your front, too!"

"Gee, if these guys start popping up without me even having to touch stuff…" Cori began.

"Your life will never be boring!" Marta laughed.

"Yeah, no doubt," Cori laughed back. "I think we should go back to the last room where we saw the Amazon. See if she'll pop in for a visit."

"What if the conquistadors show up?" Marta said. "Those guys hate what the Amazon did to them. They definitely have a revenge thing working. They may not be particular about which woman they kill. After nearly 500 hundred years of looking for a kill, any female might do – like YOU."

"Maybe. But we need to see if the Amazon will come back. There may be more she can show us that will help," argued Cori.

"Well, ok. But this time…" Marta began.

"I know. I know. Cameras!" Cori laughed.

"Good," Marta laughed back. "I don't want to miss any more of the action. I hate hearing ghost stories secondhand."

———————

Cori slowly opened the door and peaked inside.

Not a conquistador ghost in sight.

She walked to a table lined with skulls.

"Last time, touching a human skull seemed to have gotten her attention. Maybe we should try it again," Cori said. "Which one do you think?"

"Like I should know?" Marta teased. "I'm the techie. You're the expert on the dead. Can't you get a vibe or something off of one of them?"

"Been studying up on vibes, have you?" laughed Cori.

"Need for knowledge," answered Marta. "You know, the energy of a spirit that gets locked inside an object that the ghost owned or that meant a lot to them. You're a ghost hunter. Can't you pick up on vibes?"

"You'd think so, wouldn't you?" Cori laughed at Marta's question. "I've never tried it but now seems to be a pretty good time to see what I can pick up on."

Cori picked up a skull.

"Hmm, no vibe here," she said, returning it to the table. "How about that skull with the hole? Looks like someone hit him with a baseball bat."

"Maybe a club with a rock on the end," Marta joked. "I don't think baseball was invented by either the conquistadors or the Amazons!"

"Nope, not a single vibe," Cori announced, placing the skull back down on the table. "See any other possible vibe-filled skulls I should touch?"

"Nope," concluded Marta. "They all pretty much look alike. Just touch 'em all. Let the ghosts sort out the vibes on the other side!"

Cori continued to lift the skulls from the table. She handled each briefly before placing it back onto the table. Quietly, behind her, a haze began to form.

"We have ghosts! Haze forming over your right shoulder," Marta warned. "I can't make it out. Don't know if it's friend or foe."

Cori turned quickly. She peered into the haze. She watched as the outline of the ghost began to appear.

"It's ok," Cori reported to Marta. "Nobody here but us Amazons."

Cori gently put the skull she was holding back onto the table. The ghost of the Amazon moved slowly across the room. Her eyes focused on Cori as she moved closer to the table. Cori stood frozen in place.

The camera on the bill of Cori's cap sent the image of the Amazon's face onto Marta's computer screen.

"Whoa!" whispered Marta. "Look at those eyes! Feel like she's staring right through you? Think, maybe, she doesn't trust you?"

"I think, maybe, she doesn't know yet," Cori

whispered back. "But, with that blowgun slung over her shoulder, I'm not making any sudden moves – like waving hello!"

The ghost of the Amazon warrior picked up the skull Cori had just laid down. Immediately, the room began to change.

"Guess that was the one with the vibe," Marta laughed softly.

"Guess so," agreed Cori.

The haze around the ghost turned into a mist.

"It suddenly feels damp," Cori reported to Marta. "And cold."

"So, we get to see the rain forest vision again?" Marta asked as the image of a vision began to display on her monitor.

"Yeah, it's a vision, but not the same one as before," answered Cori. "Different skull, different vision."

Cori and Marta watched as the energy of the Amazon ghost was pulled headlong into the vision. Again, standing alone in the basement, Cori felt a chill come over her body.

"Well, that sure explains why you're feeling cold and damp!" exclaimed Marta, staring at the images of the vision. "And it explains a lot about the Amazon ghost."

To see what surprised Marta,

go to the webscene at:

www.TheGhostHunterOnline.com/webscene2-7

"So that was the image the Amazon saw as she was dying," Cori said softly, remembering the ghost who only moments before had stood a few feet from her.

"I'd hate for that to be the last thing I ever saw," Marta offered. "What an awful thing to have stuck in your mind for eternity! Like drowning isn't bad enough! To be trying to reach the surface, gasping for air… and, then, see that."

"Well, at least it gives us a good idea of what is holding her here," Cori said, watching the last of the images fade as the vision disappeared.

"It does?" asked Marta surprised.

"Yeah," said Cori. "You said it in your email."

"I did?" Marta's surprise turning to confusion. "I must be so smart! What was it exactly that I said?"

"You said our ghost was a real hero to her people.

What if she was a hero but never knew it!" Cori said, excitement growing in her voice.

"Ok, stop!" Marta replied. "You're really getting me confused here. How could she not know she was a hero? After the fight, the tribes down the river began to fight back. The conquistadors were afraid to go near Amazon land. That was ALL because of the courage of the Amazon queen leading them into battle."

"Yeah. AFTER the fight the conquistadors were afraid to go near land. AFTER the fight the tribes had the courage to fight back. All that happened AFTER the fight because of what the Amazon queen did. But the queen never knew any of that," Cori answered.

"Because she was already dead," interrupted Marta. "She never even saw the rest of the battle. She couldn't possibly have known that she had inspired other tribes to have the courage to fight. Tribal elders probably told stories about her bravery! How she was fighting two and three soldiers at a time! And, how, even as she was falling from the ship, she grabbed the enemy and took them overboard with her. With all the armor they were wearing, the conquistadors must have sunk straight to the bottom of the river! To her people, I bet she was more than just a hero. I bet she was a legend!"

"Maybe," agreed Cori. "But, in her mind, she died a coward."

"A coward? Ok, maybe not knowing she was a hero, I can see. But, why would she think that she was a coward?" Marta tried to understand.

"Well, for an Amazon warrior – especially a queen – the only honorable death would have been death on the battlefield, alongside her warriors," Cori explained.

"Ok. So, since she fell over the side of the ship, drowning when the current pulled her under, she thinks she died a coward," Marta reasoned. "Just because she didn't die beside her warriors."

"The worst thing to a warrior is to die without honor," Cori said. "So… if everyone thought I was a hero but I thought I was a coward…"

"Then, in your own mind, you'd still be a coward?"

Marta replied. "It's always what you think of yourself that matters most."

"Uh-huh. And if you're a warrior and didn't think you died with honor…" Cori added.

"You'd be stuck here, unable to cross over to the other side!" they both shouted together.

"That makes it a guilt thing, right?" Marta reasoned. "She feels guilty about not dying with her warriors."

"That would be the simple answer," Cori began.

"Please, with you, nothing is ever simple." Marta joked. "So what's ruining our perfectly simple solution?"

"The conquistadors," Cori replied.

"Ah, them again!" Marta laughed, but then became more serious. "You're right. The conquistadors! The Amazon might feel guilty. But those guys never felt guilty about anything! Not stealing. Destroying homes. Killing entire villages of people! No guilt holding those souls to the earth!"

"Nope," agreed Cori. "So, it's hard to imagine how they and the Amazon could share any bond of guilt –

much less one strong enough to bind them together for 500 years."

"Well, the only other thing they have in common is that they died in the same battle," reasoned Marta.

"What if these are the guys she pulled overboard with her?" Cori said excitedly, realizing she had just discovered the answer.

"That's it!" agreed Marta. "If the conquistador ghosts are the guys she yanked into the river, then they died exactly when she died!"

"Which means that their energies are locked together in the very same moment of time!" Cori explained. "That's what they have in common! The moment of death! But one thing I still don't get is how did they end up here in California thousands of miles from South America?"

"That's easy," Marta said. "Remember how I said the Amazon River goes almost all the way across the continent of South America?"

"Yeah," Cori said.

"It's like the way the Mississippi River goes north and south, almost dividing the United States in half. It flows south and then empties into the Gulf of Mexico," Marta explained. "If you put a message in a bottle and drop it into the water near where the Mississippi River starts, the current will carry it all the way down the river to the Gulf of Mexico."

"You're right. That must be what happened to the Amazon queen and the conquistadors," Cori agreed. "They fell into the river like a message in a bottle. Their bodies floated downstream. The Amazon River empties into the Atlantic Ocean. Then it was just a matter of time and ocean currents before the ghosts all ended up on the coast of California."

"So, for 500 hundreds years, they have been bouncing around on the waves, fighting each other?" Marta concluded.

"Probably. Doesn't appear they have worked out their differences and become friends," Cori joked, knowing the ghosts cannot change their reality but are forever locked into reliving their true actions. "But, when the team from the dig brought back all those artifacts…"

"The sudden presence of things that they were so closely connected to in life messed with their energy! They started feeling their energy drawn to things in the museum and the rest we know," Marta smiled to herself as she put together the last piece to the puzzle.

"They have been battling for almost 500 years," Cori summed up. "And they'll keep on fighting the same battle, unless…"

"Unless we come up with a way to convince the Amazon that she's a hero. If we do that, she can move on, finally leaving behind the conquistadors she was unfortunate enough to die with! Imagine the pain and suffering that will cause them! Eternity with no one to fight! But, how can we convince the Amazon that she didn't die in disgrace?" Marta wondered aloud.

"Hmm. Convincing a ghost that she died with honor," Cori said. "Not as easy as it first might appear."

"Strange, I didn't think it sounded easy at all! Just

think how hard it seems to me!" Marta laughed weakly at the huge task before them. "Where do we begin?"

"We know the conquistadors came to villages along the Amazon River and attacked them," Cori began.

"And our Amazon queen saw them attack a village," Marta added.

"After that, she must have gone back and warned her own village. That's how they were ready when the boats came," Cori continued.

"They fought. And the Amazon died trying to fight for her people," Marta finished. "Don't know what else there is."

"I don't either," Cori told her. "The only thing is if there's anything else in the museum we haven't found yet."

"We've been over every bone, skull and skin in the place!" Marta said exhaustedly. "What could possibly be left?"

"There's still one room left," Cori offered. "It's at the end of the hall. Maybe it has something."

"The something better be a miracle!" Marta replied.

———————

Cori walked down the long hallway. She stopped outside the one door behind which she had not yet explored. Slowly, Cori opened the next door.

"Oh, cool!" Marta exclaimed as the first images of the room appeared on her monitor. "Masks!"

Images streamed across Marta's monitor as the cameras slowly scanned around the room. Masks of every description hung on the walls. Some were clay, painted bright colors. Others were carved from wood. Still others were made from the bones and skins of animals.

Some were short and would cover only a small part of a person's head. Others were large, with empty eyeholes staring into the room.

"Masks are so cool" came Marta's voice. "They've been around for at least 20,000 years. Almost every culture has used masks at one time or another. Some use masks in religious ceremonies. Others wore them into battle. Some masks represent gods. Lots of masks are made to look like animals with skins or feathers. People wanted to have the animal's power. So they wore a mask that looked like the animal."

"When we first saw the Amazon at the beach she was wearing a mask," Cori reminded her sidekick.

"That's right!" Marta agreed. "It'd make sense – wearing a mask when she went into battle. She probably had a special mask since she was the queen. But, these masks could have been worn by her warriors. This is great stuff, but I don't know how it's going to help us."

Cori picked up a mask from one of the tables. Quietly, the Amazon warrior faded into view.

"Ok, it's the ol' vibe and vision thing again," Cori smiled to herself.

"Don't get too happy too fast," Marta warned. "She's not alone – and neither are you!"

Cori turned to look behind her. The conquistadors had once again appeared. And Cori was smack in the middle between them and the Amazon!

One of the conquistadors raised his gun.

The Amazon pulled a single arrow out and placed it in her bow.

"Gun vs. wooden arrow. Here, let me guess who's going to win!" Cori reasoned. "The Amazon hasn't got a chance!"

"I wouldn't count her out yet!" came Marta's encouragement. "Looks like backup just arrived!"

To see what suddenly appeared in the room, go to the webscene at:
www.TheGhostHunterOnline.com/webscene2-8

Chapter Nine

"Come back and fight, you cowards!" Cori laughed.

"Looks like the big, brave conquistadors don't want to fight unless they have a sure win. Did you see the way they turned and ran? The look on their faces! They'd be scared to death if they weren't already dead!" Marta joined in the laughter.

"Yeah, but it's a good thing they took off so quickly," began Cori. "Because the ghosts of the warriors have left the building!"

"You're kidding!" Marta exclaimed in disbelief.

Cori slowly looked around the room. The cameras sent images back to Marta. Not a single warrior ghost came into view. The masks were once again only masks on a wall. The ghost of the Amazon warrior queen was gone, too.

"Aw, gee!" Cori showed her disappointment. "I'm here all alone again! What are we going to do now?"

"First thing we have to do is get everybody back together again. Everybody but the conquistadors," Marta replied. "I've got an idea."

"I'm all ears! What's the idea?" Cori replied.

"It seems this room has more energy in it than any of the others we have been in," Marta began. "I mean, everyone showed up! Even warriors who never appeared before!"

"Probably had to do with the masks," Cori reasoned. "If they were wearing them in battle when they died, the masks would be able to draw their energy to this place."

"If we could draw enough of their energy to this place, could we help them bring a vision of something that happened in their lives?" Marta asked the ghost expert.

"Seems possible," Cori thought about the idea. "What do you have in mind?"

"Wouldn't the warriors have worn the masks at other times besides in battle?" Marta asked.

"Sure," Cori answered. "Really special times like when the tribe crowned a queen…"

"Or buried a queen!" Marta interrupted.

"Amazons didn't bury. They burned," Cori continued. "But, yeah, you're right. They would have had a ceremony. Placed the body upon a pile of wood and burned it. It's called a funeral pyre. This would have released the spirit of the dead to travel over to the other side in honor."

"And if the person had died in disgrace?" Marta asked knowingly.

"They wouldn't have gotten a funeral pyre," Cori answered. "What are you getting at?"

"The ghosts of the warriors were pulled into the masks when the conquistadors showed up. That was because their energies were drawn to the masks they had worn in battle. The conquistadors made that pull greater by combining two experiences at once – the masks for battle, plus, they were the enemy," Marta tried to explain.

"Ok, with you so far," Cori laughed softly.

"So, if we created another moment in the warriors'

85

lives, add some artifacts from that moment to help pull their energy in the same way the conquistadors did…" Marta continued.

"Then, the ghosts of the warriors would return in that moment of their lives," Cori finished her sidekick's explanation. "Probably living out the moment in a vision!"

"Exactly!" exclaimed Marta.

"What moment are we shooting for?" Cori asked.

"The funeral pyre of the Amazon queen!" Marta answered. "Her warriors did not have her body to burn. It washed away down the river. But, they would have wanted to send her spirit off to the place of honor, right? So, they would have gathered all the things she needed for the journey…"

"And had a funeral pyre!" Cori said excitedly. "Marta, you're a genius!"

"Let's hope so," Marta answered softly. "The spirit of the ghost of the Amazon warrior queen depends on it! I just hope these ghosts didn't die in the same battle as our Amazon queen. If they did, it won't work. They wouldn't have lived long enough to honor the death of the queen."

"But, if they survived the battle in which the queen died," Cori tried to sound hopeful. "Then, the funeral pyre honoring the queen would be a moment in their lives that they could return to."

"Creating a vision that we can see," Marta continued. "And, if we can see the vision, the ghost of the Amazon queen can see it, too."

"Guess the rest is up to me," Cori concluded. "I'll gather up some of the artifacts in the room. Things the dead would have needed to take with them for their journey to the other side."

Cori walked around the room, moving from one artifact to another. A bow with several arrows beside it. A blowgun. A clay bowl and other utensils. A pair of moccasins. A conquistador's helmet. She carried them over to an empty table near the masks hanging on the wall. She laid the items down and stepped away.

"Think that's enough?" Marta asked, watching

Cori's efforts via her monitor.

"Guess we'll find out soon enough," Cori replied, walking back to stand next to the mask that had brought the ghost of the Amazon queen.

"YES!" Marta yelled in a whisper. "Here they come!"

The masks again rose from the wall. A glow formed around each one. Slowly, the forms of the women warriors came into view. The warriors moved toward the items that Cori had placed on the table. One warrior placed her hand above the bow and arrows which then rose in the air. Another stretched her hand over the blowgun which also rose into the air. The warriors continued to take a place by the table until all of the artifacts were floating in the air.

"It's working," Cori whispered to Marta. "Here comes the mist."

The mist of a vision filled the room. It drifted around the masked warriors.

"The vision is taking their energy," Cori described the scene for her friend. "There they go into the vision."

"Is it a vision of a funeral pyre?" Marta struggled to see through the haze on her screen.

"Yeah," Cori whispered. "It's a funeral pyre. Guess it's time to call the Queen."

Cori picked up the mask that had earlier summoned the ghost of the Amazon queen to appear. Like before, the Amazon appeared in a mist. She neared Cori, stretching her hand out toward the mask.

Cori slowly moved the mask toward the vision taking place on the other side of the room. The Amazon queen turned to follow the direction of the mask. As she did, she became aware of the vision.

"Does she see it?" Marta asked quietly.

"Yes," Cori whispered back. "She sees her warriors at a funeral pyre. Does she know it's her funeral pyre? We'll know in a minute."

Cori and Marta watched as the ghost of the Amazon warrior queen watched the vision. She watched as each warrior placed an item on the huge pile of wood. The bow and arrows to help the dead kill food for her journey. The blowgun to kill old enemies she might happen to meet. The clay bowl and other utensils to prepare food as well as offerings to the gods. The moccasins to begin walking the new road of her journey on the other side.

The ghost of the Amazon queen watched closely.

"Anything?" Marta asked.

"Nope," Cori replied. "She doesn't seem to know that it's her funeral."

The last masked warrior climbed to the top of the pile. She placed the conquistador's helmet atop all the other items. Suddenly, the ghost of the queen moved closer to the vision. She stared at the top of the pile of wood. She stared at the conquistador's helmet.

"The helmet would represent a conquered enemy," Marta whispered. "She's realizing that the conquistadors were defeated. But, if she doesn't figure out the funeral is hers, will knowing she helped defeat the enemy be enough to free her?"

"Doesn't matter," Cori replied, her smile could be

heard in her voice. "Look at that!"

Marta watched the images on her monitor.

The last masked warrior returned to the ground from atop the pile of wood. Then, she bowed her head. One by one, all the warriors bowed their heads. Finally, all the warriors dropped down on one knee.

"They're bowing!" Marta cried out. "Yes! Now she has to know they are honoring a queen! They wouldn't bow to another warrior. They would bow only to a queen! And THIS queen had conquered the enemy!"

"She understands," Cori reported, observing the ghost standing near her. "She realizes that she died with honor and the respect of her warriors. Her spirit is finally free to pass over into the next world. And she's not wasting any time."

Marta watched the vision fade slowly from her screen.

"Safe journey, warrior," she whispered.

You can see the pyre, too. Go to the webscene at:
www.TheGhostHunterOnline.com/webscene2-9

91

Wish you could use **Ghost Hunter** books
in your classroom?

Maybe you can.

Tell your teacher that each **Ghost Hunter** book
has a FREE online teacher guide that
includes suggestions for classroom activities.

Ask your teacher to visit
www.TheGhostHunterOnline.com
and click on

"TEACHER GUIDES"